For the real Zachary and his sister, Amy — L.G.

For Neddy, with love — J.J.

First published in the United States 2001
by Phyllis Fogelman Books
An imprint of Penguin Putnam Books for Young Readers
345 Hudson Street
New York, New York 10014

Published in Great Britain as *When I Grow Up*
by Macmillan Children's Books
Text copyright © 2000 by Lennie Goodings
Illustrations copyright © 2000 by Jenny Jones

Printed in Belgium

1 3 5 7 9 10 8 6 4 2

Library of Congress Cataloging-in-Publication
Data available upon request

WHEN YOU GROW UP

by Lennie Goodings

illustrated by Jenny Jones

Phyllis Fogelman Books
New York

Zachary and his mom
have the same color fur
and the same color eyes.

They both like to hug and they both like
chocolate ice cream with honey on top.
In the morning they are both yawning,
sleepy-eyed sleepyheads.
  Zachary says, when he grows up,
he's going to live with his mom.
        Mom says that's all right with her.
                    But . . .

"Maybe," says Mom, "when you grow up, you'll be a famous soccer star."

"Oh, yes!" says Zachary. "I will score all the goals and be a hero! And then I'll come back and live with you."

"Or maybe," says Mom,
"when you grow up,
you might be a baker."

"Mmm!" says Zachary. "And I'll make sticky chocolate birthday cakes every single day."

"Will you let me lick the bowl?" asks Mom.

"I might." Zachary laughs. "And then I'll come back and live with you."

"Maybe," says Mom, "when you grow up, you'll be a pilot and fly a helicopter."

"That will be great," says Zachary.

"I'll go high up over the clouds."

"Oh, yes!" says Mom.

"And then I'll come back and live with you."

"Or maybe," says Mom, "you'll be an ambulance driver and save someone's life."

"Yes!" says Zachary. "And I'll zoom through the streets with the siren going and the lights flashing. And then I'll come back and live with you."

"Or maybe," says Mom, "you'll be a cowboy and ride a big horse."

"Yippee," says Zachary. "And I'll lasso cows with a rope.

"And then I'll be made sheriff and I'll have a shiny star and a big hat."

"Oooh!" says Mom.

"And I'll catch all the bad guys
and throw them in jail," says
Zachary. "And then I'll come
back and live with you."

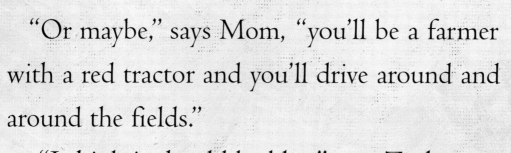

"Or maybe," says Mom, "you'll be a farmer with a red tractor and you'll drive around and around the fields."

"I think it should be blue," says Zachary.

"Oh?" says Mom.

"Yes, blue, because that's my favorite color!

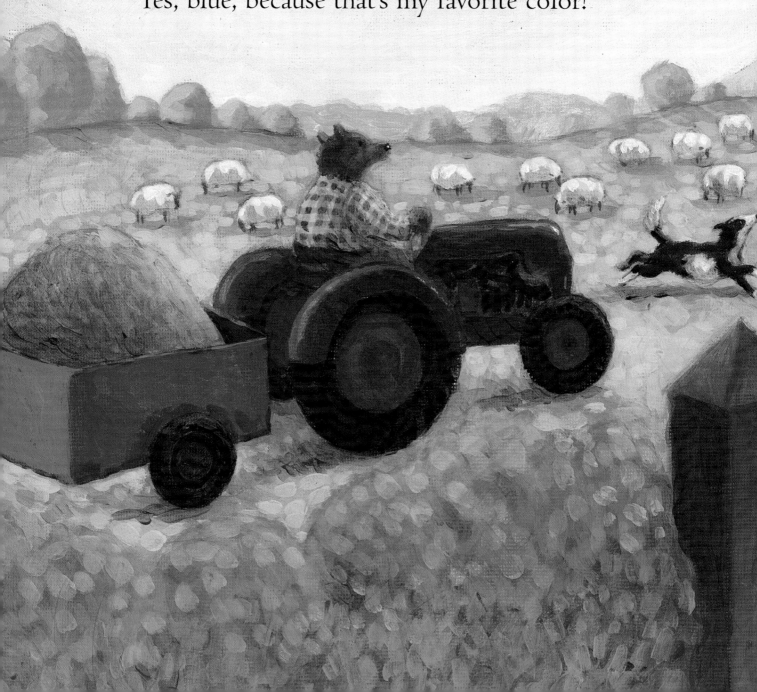

"And I'll have a big friendly dog and he'll help me look after my sheep," says Zachary. "And then I'll come back and live with you."

"Or maybe," says Mom, "you'll be a
magician and make rabbits jump out of hats."

"Oh, yes!" says Zachary. "I will make
you disappear!"

"Oh, no!" says Mom.

"But I'll make you appear again. And then
I'll come back and live with you."

"Maybe," says Mom, "you'll be a daddy and have a little cub just like you."

"I might . . ." says Zachary. "And then . . .

"we'll all live next door to you!"